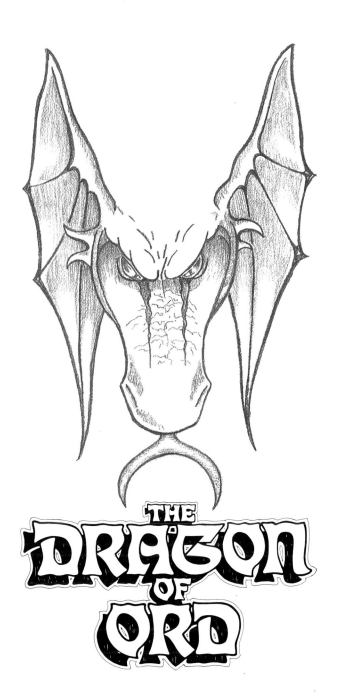

THE DRAGON OF ORD

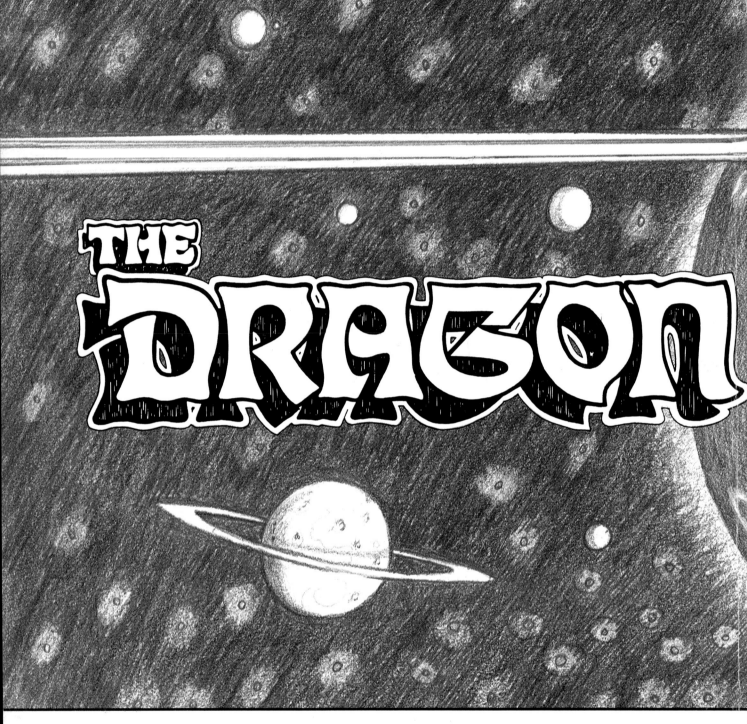

International Standard Book Number: 0-933849-02-8
Library of Congress Catalog Card Number: 85-81417

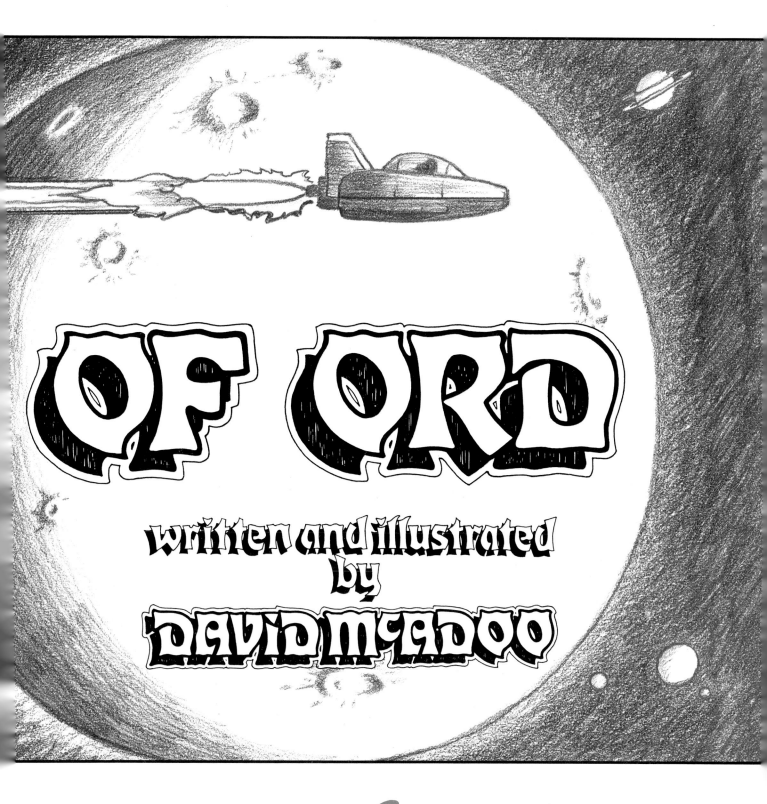

OF ORD

written and illustrated by
DAVID McADOO

LANDMARK EDITIONS, INC.

1420 Kansas Avenue • Kansas City, Missouri 64127
(816) 241-4919

PROLOGUE

It is the year 6024 A.D. — three thousand years after the Great Intergalactic War. Mighty nations of the world are gone. People have forgotten all forms of science and once again believe in sorcery and magic.

Some stories tell how the Prince of Darkness, the evil one called Argos, stole the world's technological knowledge and spirited it into outer space. Others maintain Argos was killed when his spaceship was drawn into the never-ending depths of the Black Hole of the Universe. People pray Argos will never return, but they fear that someday he might.

Our planet is no longer called Earth. It is known as Ord. The world is now divided into small kingdoms that are dependent upon their supplies of gold for survival. Kings protect stockpiles of gold at all costs, for any king who loses the gold forfeits his right to rule.

Such is the setting for our story of monstrous deeds and great heroics — a story some may deny, but deep in their hearts they know it happened exactly as it is told.

THE STORY BEGINS

In a small hut in the Eastern Kingdom of Galatia, a baby was born. A soothsayer told the child's parents their son would grow to become the greatest of the warriors and possess the purest heart of all. The proud parents named the baby, Flare.

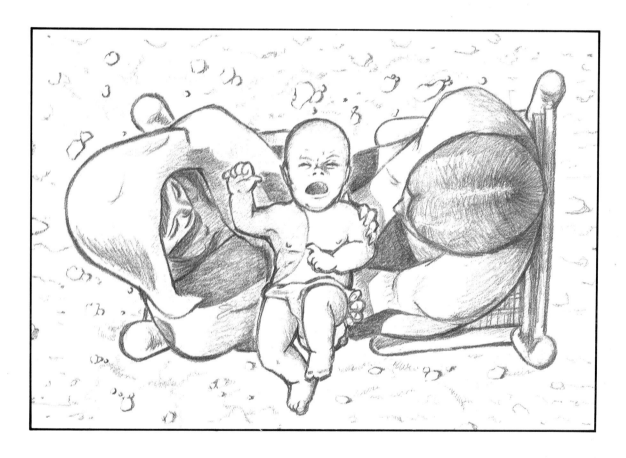

At the instant of Flare's birth — in a distant galaxy, a laser beam was shot from a spaceship. The ray of light pierced the starry darkness as it hurled a mysterious egglike object through the region known as the Ancient Sea of Silent Threats.

Although the strange egg was propelled seven times faster than the speed of light, it would take nearly twenty years for it to travel the great distance. The missile sped toward its ultimate target — the unsuspecting Kingdom of Galatia on the Planet Ord.

1

Unaware of the evil forces at work, good King Oric, ruler of the Kingdom of Galatia, stepped outside his castle gates to take his early morning walk. It was a beautiful, clear day. The sun shone brightly and the king was in a mood of peaceful contentment.

Suddenly the sky turned black as night. King Oric was startled by the sound of thunder and the jagged flash of light that struck the ground nearby — a light so brilliant the old man was momentarily blinded by its intensity.

When he regained his sight, he saw before him an egg that gleamed amber in color, then changed to green. The king watched in terror and amazement as the egg glowed with the white heat of a burning star. When its metallic shell split open, he saw something green and alive move within. Then out slithered a tiny dragon, hissing angrily and clawing the air. The terrified king gasped in horror as the beast flapped its pointed wings and flames of fire spewed from its nostrils.

The creature began to grow in size at an astonishing rate of speed. With each flap of its wings, the beast grew larger and its flames burst forth with increasing heat and fury. At last the dragon stood one hundred feet tall.

Although King Oric summoned his army to protect the castle, their weapons were powerless against the dragon's strength and size. With one mighty kick of its hind legs, the beast made splinters of the castle door. Going on a rampage, it thrashed through the castle halls until it found the chamber where the kingdom's riches were stored. Hissing with greedy pleasure, the dragon bent down, scooped up all the gold coins, and packed them in its massive cheeks and under its slimy tongue.

Then bellowing loudly, the beast spread its wings, and with the force of titans it bolted straight up, crashed through the chamber ceiling and flew out of the castle.

Except for a few coins the dragon had carelessly dropped and left behind, the inner chamber had been stripped of its treasure — the gold was gone!

"My kingdom is lost!" sobbed King Oric, for he was aware that without the gold, he was no more than a peasant who would be forced to declare bankruptcy. His family's name would be disgraced. He knew of some kings who had been so ashamed of losing their kingdoms that they changed their names and moved out of town. Now, he would have to do the same.

The king was distraught. The grand wizard and the guards tried to console him, but it was useless. Even the court jester could not bring a smile to the old man's face.

Finally regaining control of his senses, the king realized there was only one hope for retrieving the gold. He summoned the most honored knight in the land, a free-lance warrior who had served the kingdom well on special missions.

This mighty warrior was one of great strength and purity of heart. For his bravery in slaying the Demons of Daggett, he had earned the magic Sword of Aron. His good deeds were legion. His victories were legend. His name was Flare!

Since the dragon had crammed its mouth full of more gold than it could hold, golden coins had dropped out as the beast had flown away.

Flare followed the trail of gold across the Desert of Bones and over the windswept Mountains of Forgotten Sorrows. Finally, in the Wastelands of Distant Terrors, Flare caught sight of the dragon.

The creature hovered high above the land, as if it were waiting for <u>something</u> or <u>someone</u> to arrive. <u>What</u> or <u>who</u> the dragon expected, Flare did not know, but he had to find out.

After several hours, the beast suddenly stopped in midair and looked toward the Sun. At first Flare could not see what had attracted the dragon's attention, but then he heard the roar of engines and saw a spaceship slash through the cloudless sky. As the ship landed, the dragon suddenly swooped to the ground.

To get a closer look, Flare climbed to the top of Boulder Bluff. It was then he saw a shadowy figure emerge from the spaceship. There before the dragon stood the Prince of Darkness — the evil Argos. He was not dead. He had not been trapped in the endless vacuum of the Black Hole. He was alive! And now he had returned to Ord to collect the gold he had sent the beast to steal. Only Argos could have devised such a fiendish scheme.

As Flare looked on, Argos raised his arms and commanded the obedient dragon to spit out the gold from its cavernous mouth.

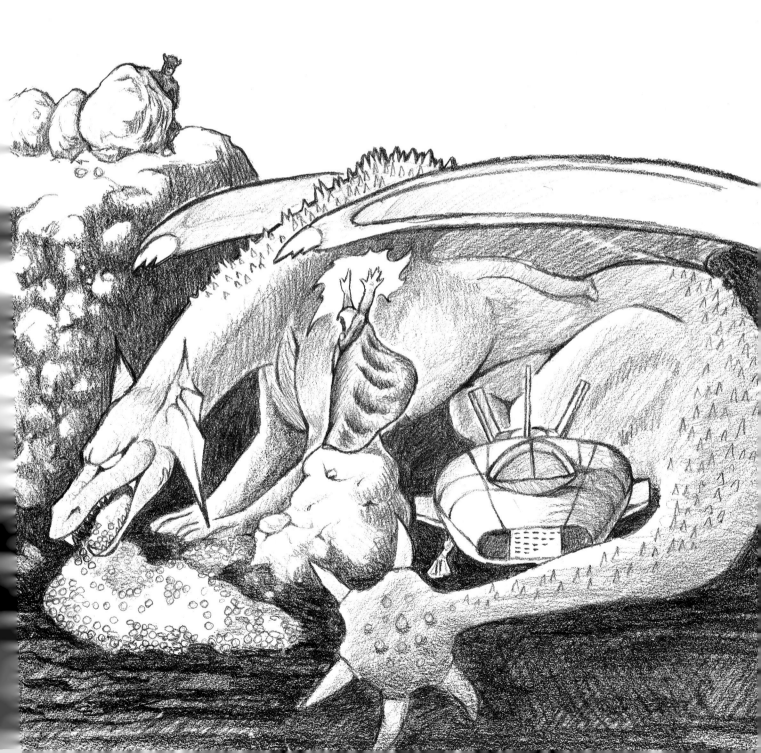

As the evil Argos ran his fingers through the stolen gold, he smiled with greed and the stench of rancid demons filled the air around him. His horrible howls of triumph echoed the wails of lost souls. The reverberating sounds grew louder and louder, inflicting great pain on Flare's mortal ears.

Fearing he would lose his senses, Flare pressed his hands against his ears, but he could not shut out the unbearable noise.

Knowing he must stop the sounds before they destroyed his mind, Flare pushed his hands against a huge boulder, and with all his might he tried to move it. The stone would not budge. He tightened his muscles and tried again. Nothing happened — the boulder was too heavy.

Desperately summoning even more of his strength, Flare pressed all of his energy and all of his thought against the stone.

"Move!" he commanded mentally, as he pushed even harder.

At first the boulder vibrated only slightly. Then responding to Flare's strength and determination, the great rock began to roll toward the rim of the cliff. With one last powerful surge, it went over the edge and crashed below, almost striking the dragon's head and just missing the evil Argos.

11

Using the element of surprise to his advantage, Flare leaped from the cliff onto the dragon's gigantic head. Rearing its head high in the air, the beast tried to throw off its attacker, but in defiance, Flare pressed his legs tightly against the monster and struggled to hold fast.

Pulling the Sword of Aron from its scabbard and calling upon all the magic it possessed, Flare raised it above his head and brought it down with the mightiest of blows, sending the dragon plummeting to the ground.

Jumping from the lifeless body of the slain dragon, the courageous Flare turned to confront the evil Argos. But as Flare prepared to wield a mortal blow, Argos unleashed his awesome powers of blinding light and instantly translocated himself to safety inside his spaceship.

As the spaceship of Argos blasted off, Flare raised his sword and cried out, "O'cowardly demon, come back and fight!"

Watching the spaceship zoom toward outer space, Flare shook his head in disgust that the wicked Argos had tricked him and escaped.

Flare was relieved the gold was safe, but when he looked at the piles of coins, he realized he faced yet another problem.

"How can I carry all this gold back to the castle?" he wondered aloud.

He leaned against the fallen dragon to rest. When his hand touched the scaly skin of the beast, he thought of a splendid idea — since the dragon had stolen the gold, the beast would now assist in its return!

With his dependable sword, Flare skinned the dragon, then made several large bags from the tough hide. After filling the bags with the coins, he carried the gold to the good King of Galatia.

"How can I reward your bravery?" the joyous King Oric asked. "Just name your price."

"Money and power cannot pay for courage and honest deeds," replied Flare. "Purity of heart is its own reward."

The good king said he understood.

As Flare left the castle, he walked tall with his head held high.

EPILOGUE

While the people of Galatia cheered his brave deed, Flare realized his moment of triumph was incomplete because Argos had escaped. The mighty warrior knew that somewhere in the vastness of time and space the Prince of Darkness lurked, not content to leave well enough alone.

Flare was certain that next year or the year after that, or even perhaps in some distant century, the evil Argos would return to strike with more cunning and power than ever before.

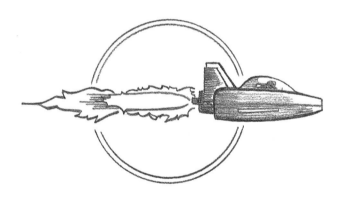

DAVID McADOO
Author and Illustrator

At ten years of age, David Sheridan McAdoo wrote and illustrated his first book, THE DRAGON OF ORD, while attending a five-day Written & Illustrated by... Workshop conducted by author/illustrator David Melton.

However, David's career in writing and illustrating really began at age three when his parents could not keep a pencil out of his hand. When he was a fifth grader, David was awarded the Springfield, Missouri Art Museum Scholarship for his first film animation, and his art work was displayed at the museum. In sixth grade, his entry won an award in a citywide poster competition sponsored by the Springfield Women's League on Crime Prevention. An honor roll student in junior high school, David was also cartoonist for the school newspaper. He has developed original designs for T-shirts for softball teams and personal business cards for his father.

David is now a fourteen-year-old freshman in high school with special interests in art and journalism. His fascination with biology led him to become an avid snake collector. He has also participated in a variety of sports — Mighty Mites football, Boys' Club basketball, and Kiwanis baseball. At present, he plays high school football.

David lives in Springfield, Missouri with his family, including two brothers and a sister. His goal is to continue to excel in art, and he dreams of the day he can afford to purchase his favorite car, a Fiero.

An Interesting Footnote

Because David's original book had been scuffed during four years of handling by interested family members and friends, and because we wanted to adapt the horizontal pages to a vertical format, we asked David to come to our offices to duplicate his illustrations. Instead of constructing mere duplications, he expanded his vision of the drawings and improved his skills, which resulted in the development of an even more extraordinary book.

For readers who are curious to see and wish to enjoy the evolvement of David's drawings, two of the original illustrations David drew at ten years of age are shown below.